and the
GREAT CHRISTMAS
RESCUE

GROSSET & DUNLAP
Published by the Penguin Group
Penguin Group (USA) LLC, 375 Hudson Street, New York, New York 10014, USA

USA | Canada | UK | Ireland | Australia | New Zealand | India | South Africa | China

penguin.com | A Penguin Random House Company

ISBN 978-0-448-48747-2   10 9 8 7 6 5 4 3 2 1

The Octopod sparkled with lights—it was nearly Christmas!

Professor Inkling had a special reason to be looking forward to Christmas this year. The Octonauts were coming home with him to celebrate!

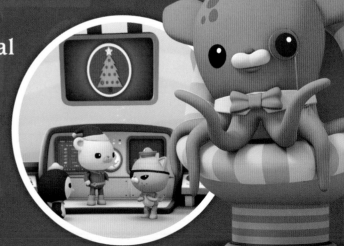

Dashi tapped a computer screen, and a picture appeared of Professor Inkling with his nephew, Squirt.

"He looks just like you," said Barnacles.

Inkling pointed to a photo of a giant rock. "This is where Squirt lives and I grew up," he explained. "The seamount."

On the seamount there were crabs, fish, sea cucumbers, and a special golden coral that was five hundred years old.

The professor's eyes twinkled.

"We all gather around her and sing a special song with the Christmas tree worms."

If the Octonauts were going to reach the seamount before the big day, they needed to get moving!

"Dashi," Barnacles commanded, "activate launch!"

Down in the launch bay, Tweak was too busy to think about celebrating. She had a top secret project to build!

Tweak's hammering and drilling echoed all the way
up the Octochute.

"I wonder what she's making," said Peso.

"Don't know, matey," replied Kwazii.

The captain chuckled. They'd just have to wait until
Christmas to find out!

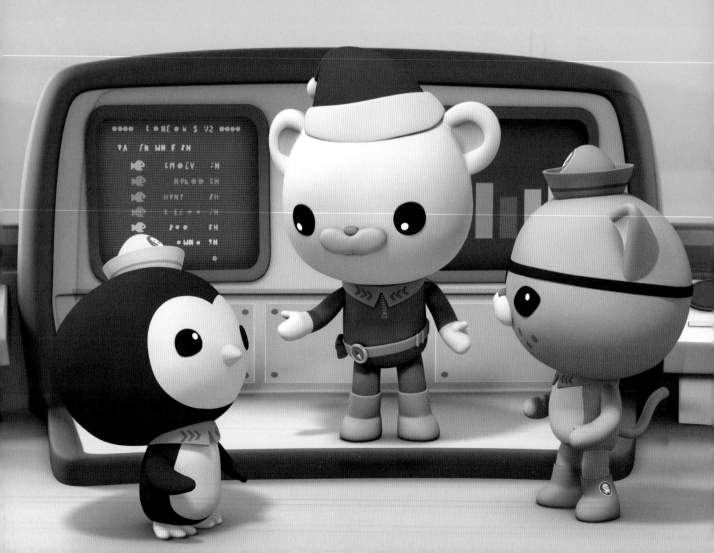

The crew had lots to do before Christmas. Kwazii helped trim the tree. When an ornament bounced into the Octochute, Kwazii slid down after it.

"What in the seven seas is that?" he gasped. A giant red machine bobbed in the water—Tweak's gift for the captain!

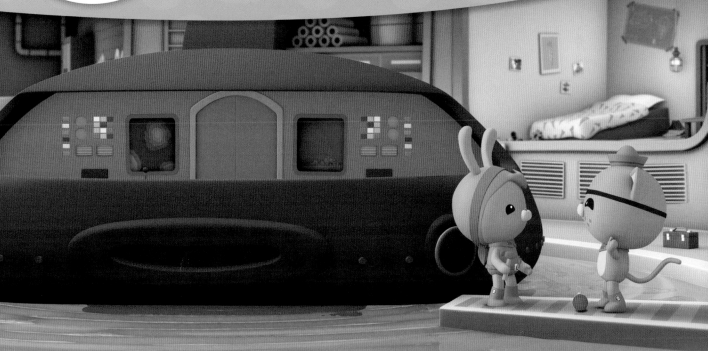

"I call it the GUP-X." She grinned. "It's the toughest GUP I've ever built!"

"That is the best present ever," whistled Kwazii, promising not to spoil the surprise.

The Octopod's voyage
was nearly over.
"There's the seamount,
Captain!" cried Dashi.
Rattle! Boom!
The vessel shuddered
and shook.

Dashi looked through the Octoscope.
"There's been some kind of rock
slide," she announced.

Dashi spun around in her chair. "That means the professor's friends and family are trapped underneath!"

"Oh no!" cried Professor Inkling. "Squirt!"

"**Sound the Octoalert!**" called Barnacles.

"**Octonauts,** to the launch **bay!**"

The Octonauts had to get the sea creatures out from under the rock pile and move them to a safe place. Professor Inkling requested permission to join the rescue. His friends and family needed him!

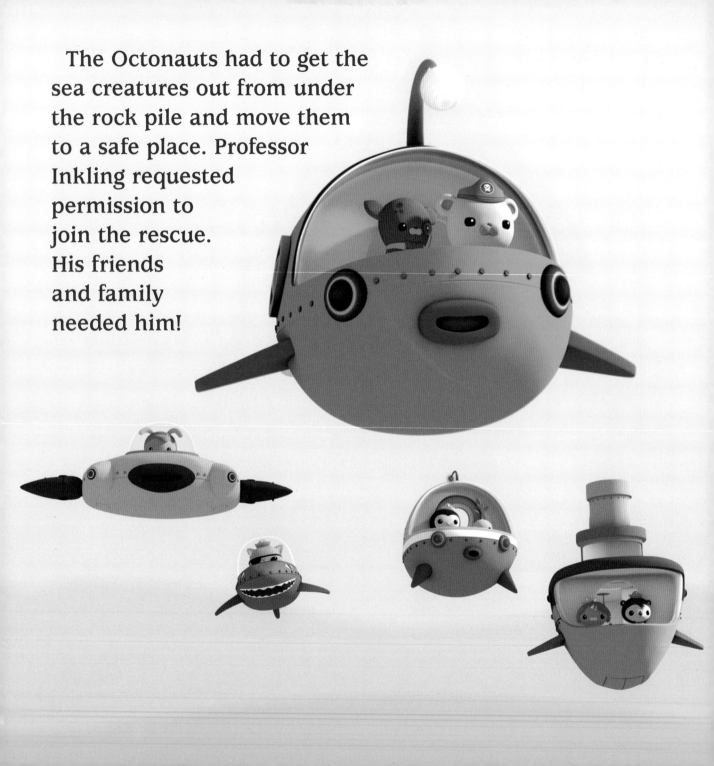

The subs rushed to the rock slide.

"Oh my," sighed the professor. "It's even bigger than we'd thought."

"On my honor as an Octonaut," Captain Barnacles promised, "we'll search until we find Squirt and all your friends. **Let's do this!**"

"Guys! Over here!"
Tweak had discovered a big round stone with a yellow tree hanging underneath it.

"That's the golden coral!" cried Professor Inkling. "Hello, old friend."

"We'll get you out and the right way up in no time," Captain Barnacles insisted.

"Dashi! We're going to need the GUP-C."

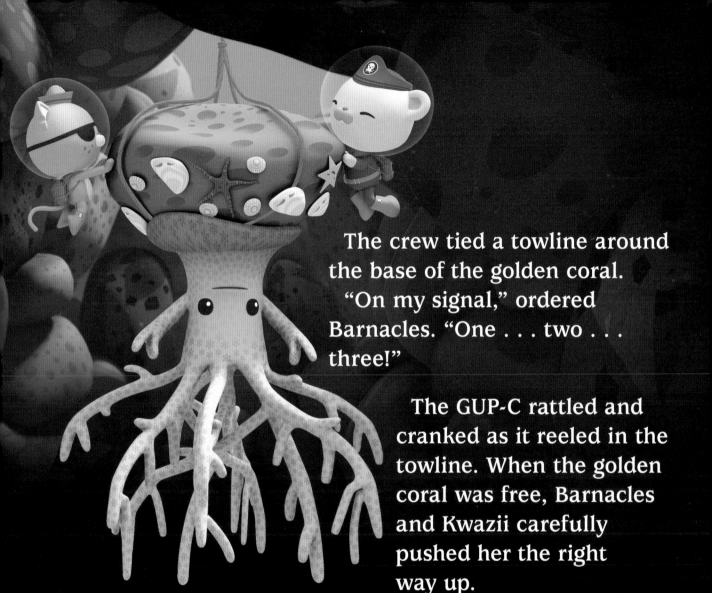

The crew tied a towline around the base of the golden coral. "On my signal," ordered Barnacles. "One . . . two . . . three!"

The GUP-C rattled and cranked as it reeled in the towline. When the golden coral was free, Barnacles and Kwazii carefully pushed her the right way up.

"Thanks for getting me out in one piece," she said, beaming.
Now only Squirt was missing.

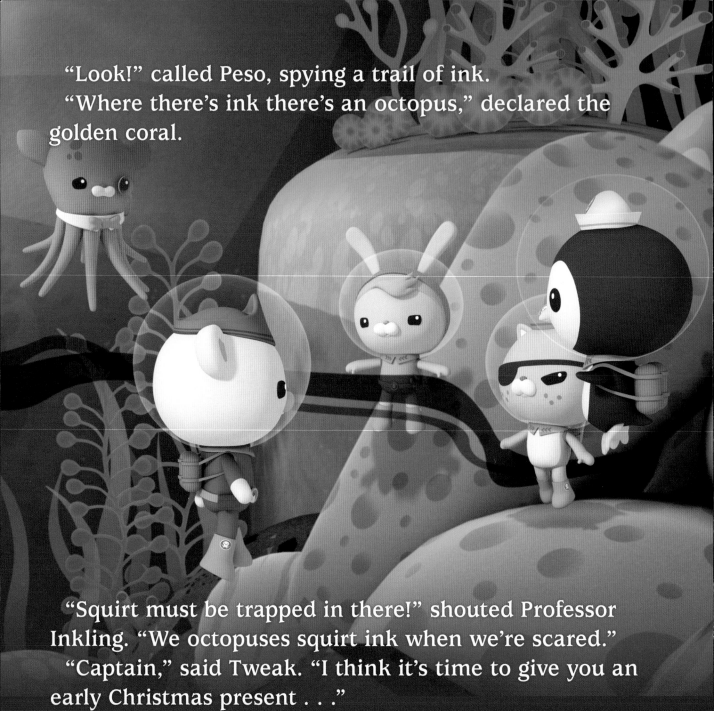

"Look!" called Peso, spying a trail of ink.

"Where there's ink there's an octopus," declared the golden coral.

"Squirt must be trapped in there!" shouted Professor Inkling. "We octopuses squirt ink when we're scared."

"Captain," said Tweak. "I think it's time to give you an early Christmas present . . ."

The brand-new GUP-X zoomed into view. It was the **toughest** GUP ever!

Captain Barnacles couldn't wait to get driving.

"Thank you!" He grinned. "This is the perfect Christmas gift at the perfect time."

The GUP-X powered through the rock slide. When the super-sub hit a dead end, Kwazii swam out to search the cave.

"More ink!" he gasped, following a curling black trail.

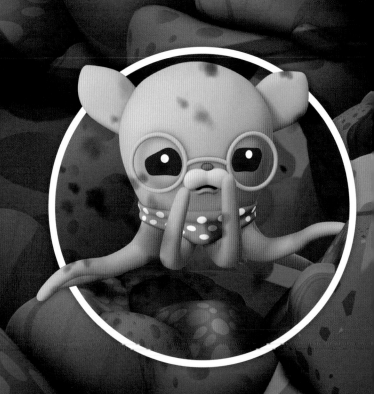

A jet of ink sploshed right into Kwazii's face. He had found Squirt!

"Sorry," whimpered the young octopus. "I'm a little scared."

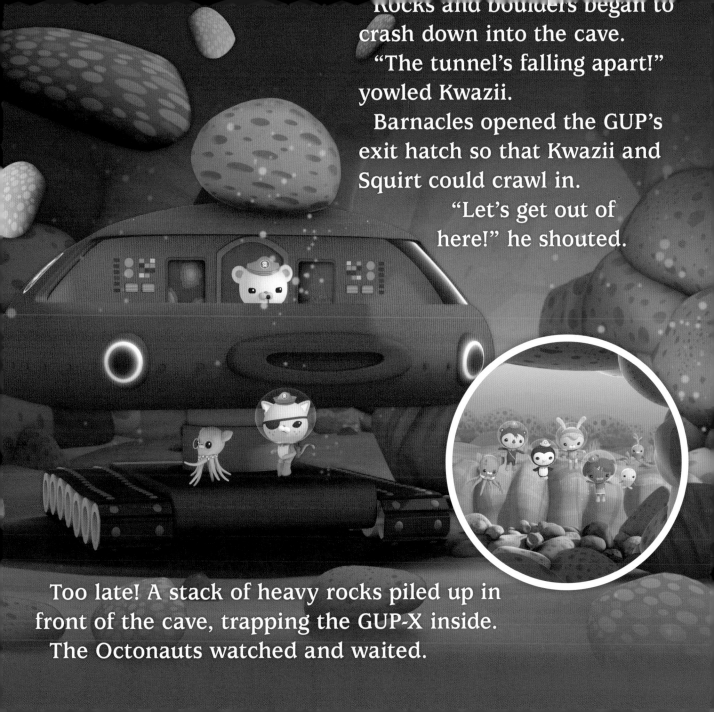

Rocks and boulders began to crash down into the cave.

"The tunnel's falling apart!" yowled Kwazii.

Barnacles opened the GUP's exit hatch so that Kwazii and Squirt could crawl in.

"Let's get out of here!" he shouted.

Too late! A stack of heavy rocks piled up in front of the cave, trapping the GUP-X inside. The Octonauts watched and waited.

Crash!

Boom!

Bang!

The GUP-X crashed its way out.
The Octonauts cheered.
"Uncle Inkling!" cried Squirt,
rushing up to give the
professor a hug.
"The gang's all here now," announced the
golden coral.

"Everybody ready up there?"
asked Captain Barnacles.
The GUP-X began to
trundle slowly up the
rock face.
"We've passed the rock
slide!" said Kwazii.
Rough water began to swirl
and bubble around the GUP-X.
It was time to operate
the sub's Octo-suction
tires!

Tweak had done a great job—the tires were working perfectly!

"Hold on," warned the captain. "Let's give these Octo-suction tires a real test."

"**Woah!**" cried the Octonauts as the sub turned upside down! The GUP-X's tires clung onto the rock face like glue.

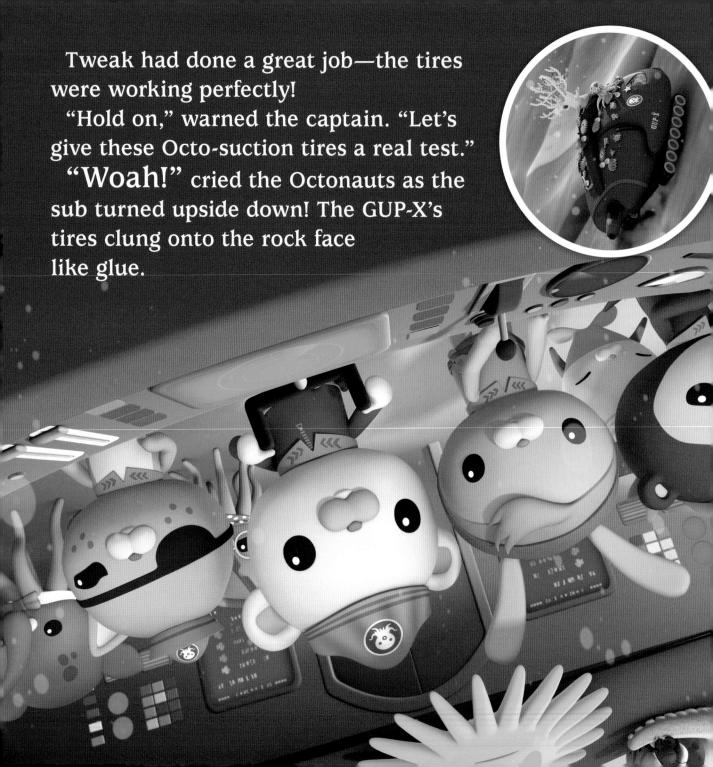

The sub was almost at the top of the seamount.

"This last climb is going to be tough," warned Barnacles. "Everyone hold on tight."

"We're ready, Captain!"

Suddenly disaster struck.

"Octonauts!" cried the golden coral.

"Sea snail overboard!"

Kwazii swam out and got the sea snail, but then the current got Kwazii! The brave pirate cat couldn't paddle back to the GUP-X.

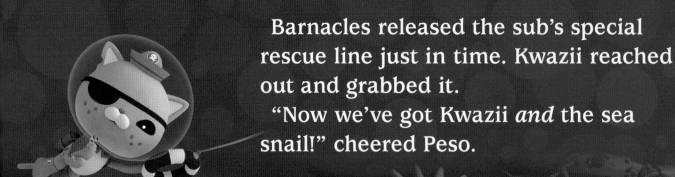

Barnacles released the sub's special rescue line just in time. Kwazii reached out and grabbed it.

"Now we've got Kwazii *and* the sea snail!" cheered Peso.

"We're almost there," announced Captain Barnacles, "but I don't think we'll make it in time for Christmas."

Tweak pointed to a special green button.

"It activates slippery slime," she explained.

The GUP-X could use slime to slide down into the middle of the seamount. Slime sliding was just like sledding!

"We made it!" said Inkling as the GUP-X slid to a stop. Peso hugged the professor. "And we're all together."

"Is it Christmas yet?" trilled the little Christmas tree worms.

Captain Barnacles pulled out his countdown clock—the happy star twinkling at the top of the tree told them it was!

The Octonauts and their friends gathered around the golden coral. "It is now," declared the captain, "finally, officially . . . Christmas!"